MYSTERY THIEF!

PUFFIN

Map of my woods

This is a map of the woods where I live. You can see who else lives here too. It's in my dad's journal, which I always have with me.

ROCKY ISLAND

OLD BROWN'S ISLAND

MR JEREMY FISHER'S POND

SQUIRREL NUTKIN'S WOOD

MRS TIGGY-WINKLE'S LAUNDRY

Cotton-tail is my littlest sister, and the naughtiest!

Squirrel Nutkin has some of the best, and nuttiest, ideas.

Mrs Tiggy-winkle runs the laundry. She keeps us neat and tidy.

This is **Mr Tod.** Foxes eat rabbits. Need I say more?

JEMIMA PUDDLE-DUCK'S HILLTOP FARM

MR MCGREGOR'S GARDEN

My friend, **Lily Bobtail.** Whatever the problem, she's got the answer.

MR TOD & TOMMY BROCK'S WOOD

MY BURROW

DR & MRS BOBTAIL'S BURROW

TUNNEL NETWORK

My mum – Mrs Rabbit to you! I try to stay on her good side.

MR BOUNCER'S BURROW (BENJAMIN'S HOME)

RAVINE

DEEP DARK WOODS

DANDELION FIELD

Benjamin Bunny is my cousin. Whatever I do, he's right behind me – usually hiding!

One sunny morning, Peter and Benjamin hopped stealthily through Mr McGregor's vegetable garden scooping up radishes.

Suddenly, Peter Rabbit stopped in his tracks, twitched his nose and pricked up his ears.

"I can hear Mr McGregor," he whispered.

"Let's hop to it!"

Peter tore off through the vegetable garden, with Benjamin close behind. Their mouths were full of stolen radishes and Mr McGregor was hot on their heels, shouting . . .

"STOP thieves!"

Just in time, the bunnies spotted a secret escape tunnel dug many years before by Peter's dad, for JUST this kind of emergency. They dived inside.

"Phew!" puffed Peter as they shot out of the other end, closely followed by 1...2...3...4 juicy radishes.

"Good job your dad dug that tunnel!"

said Benjamin when they were safely back at Peter's house.

"I hope you two haven't been getting up to mischief," Mrs Rabbit said.

"Of course not, Mum!" said Peter innocently.

The friends decided to search for somewhere else to eat their radishes.

Rushing along the path, they met Lily Bobtail
on her way to Mrs Tiggy-winkle's Laundry.
"Look what we've got, Lily,"
whispered Peter.

"RADISHES!"

gasped Lily.

"We need somewhere secret to eat them," added Benjamin. "I know just the place," she said, tucking them safely amongst the washing. "Come with me."

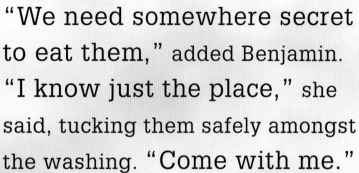

Mrs Tiggy-winkle's Laundry, high up in the hills, was the perfect secret place to eat the radishes.

"Let's get munching!" said Benjamin, rubbing his tummy.

Peter sniffed about for the secret radish stash.

"Oh no, all the baskets look the same!

After some secretive searching, three radishes were found BUT . . . there was **ONE** missing.

"Do you think we DROPPED it?" asked Peter. "Or do you think someone TOOK it?"

The three hungry rabbits retraced their steps,
in case the radish had dropped out on the path.
"There's no sign of it," said Lily.

"It must have been taken
by a mystery thief."

"We need a tip-top place to eat
the rest . . ." said Peter.

"And it doesn't get much tip-toppier than way up in the Squirrel Camp!"

"Rabbits are brave, rabbits are brave!"

Benjamin whispered to himself.

"Flippety floppety flee!
Three rabbits in a tree!"

sang silly Squirrel Nutkin when
the rabbits arrived at the top.

Reaching down, he snatched
the radishes and started
JUGGLING with them!

"Hey, Nutkin!" called Peter
desperately. "Careful with
those!" But it was too late
and the precious radishes
went whizzing past him . . .

. . . towards the ground.

"A good rabbit never gives up!"

called Peter, swinging down after the radishes as fast as he could.

Lily and Benjamin were more cautious and followed close behind in the lift.

The radishes landed in the grass
a hop and a jump away from Lily
and Benjamin, but by the time
they'd scampered to find them . . .
there was only **ONE** left.

Had the mystery thief
TAKEN the other **TWO**?

Just as they had decided to share the remaining radish, Peter felt his fur tingle, and spun around. There stood Mr Tod, **LICKING HIS LIPS.**

As the wily fox came closer, Peter spied an unusual rock.

A rock he'd seen in his dad's journal . . .

"QUICK, EVERYONE! Jump on that rock," said Peter. As the rock lifted off the ground, Peter tossed the radish at Mr Tod, shouting, "You can have our last radish, but you can't have us!"

"This was what Dad used to outfox that fox!" laughed Peter, as the rock shot away and surfed across the grass.

"Good old Dad!"

Back at the burrow, Cotton-tail
was waiting to greet the tired
and hungry bunnies.

"Hello, Cotton-tail.
What have you been
up to today?"
began Peter.

"And what's that
delicious smell?"

added Benjamin, cheering up a little.

"It smells like . . . No, it can't be."

"Radish soup!" cried Peter.

"Yes," smiled Mrs Rabbit. "Clever Cotton-tail found all these radishes."

Peter, Benjamin and Lily gasped . . . and then laughed. "Well done, Cotton-tail," giggled Peter. "Good scavenging!"

Did you guess . . .

the **MYSTERY THIEF?**

OUR SECRET BURROWS

Rabbits like us have to hide in a hurry A LOT. These old escape tunnels my dad built are perfect for a quick getaway.

Entrance (hidden under flower pot)

ONE rabbit at a time

Secret radish store

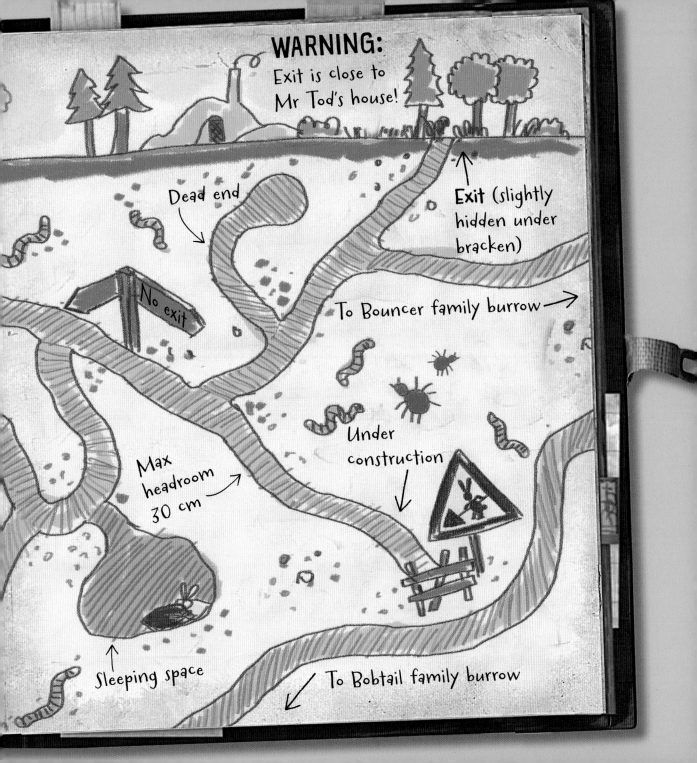

Can You SPOT While You Trot?

There are so many things to spot when you are out and about. Help us find useful things, pretty things and even tasty things. (Tasty for a rabbit, that is!)

Florence is a ladybird. I know that for a fact!

Cotton-tail spotted lots of radishes.

SEE IF YOU CAN SPOT:

- Three different shaped leaves
- A pretty flower or two
- A bird, a butterfly and a bug!

CONGRATULATIONS!

SKILL IN SPOTTING CERTIFICATE

Awarded to

_____

Age

_____

Lily Bobtail
_____

LILY BOBTAIL
BEST SPOTTER IN THE WOOD

Super
spotting
skills!